For Mum and Dad Jenkin, with love

Macmillan Publishing Company
866 Third Avenue, New York, NY 10022
First published in Great Britain in 1989 by Hutchinson
Children's Books, an imprint of Century Hutchinson Ltd
First American Edition 1989
Printed and bound in Belgium by Proost International Bookproduction

10 9 8 7 6 5 4 3 2 1

The text of this book is set in Linotron Palatino.
Design/typesetting by Roger Walker Graphic Design
ISBN 0-02-747621-9

Bad Boris
goes to school

Susie Jenkin-Pearce

Macmillan Publishing Company
New York

"Boris," said Maisie one morning, "you're old enough to go to school."

"School!" gasped Boris. "No, I'm not. I hate school!"

"Nonsense," said Maisie. "You'll do painting and writing. You'll learn to read and play lots of games. You'll *love* it!"

"No, I won't," growled Boris.

"Wish I could go," said the kitten.

But Boris just flattened his ears and refused to listen.

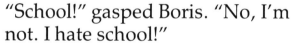

The next day they all went out to buy Boris's school things.

They bought pencils,

a pack of felt tip pens,

a painting apron,

and a lunch box.

Boris didn't even say thank you. "I hate school," was all he said.

But all young elephants must go to school, and soon it was Boris's first day.

The classroom was full of excited animals saying hello to their friends from last term, and there were some new animals looking a bit scared.

"This is Boris," said Maisie to Mrs. Prism, the teacher.

When the grown-ups had gone, Mrs. Prism called the noisy animals together. "Hush, now," she said. "You're as noisy as a class full of children."

Boris found himself next to a small crocodile who couldn't stop crying. "Don't cry," he said. "I'll look after you."

The morning went very quickly. They did painting, then music and movement.

First they pretended to be fire-breathing dragons. Then Mrs. Prism let them choose something for themselves.

"I'm a tree," cried Boris, "swaying in the breeze."

At lunchtime Boris and the crocodile shared their sandwiches. The crocodile ate one of Boris's cookies. She was already feeling a lot happier.

In the afternoon they played with sand and

water.

Mrs. Prism seemed very pleased with Boris. His trunk was just right for clearing up outside...

... and for collecting pencils.

"Boris!" said Mrs. Prism. "I don't know how I managed without you."

Back at home Maisie was having a lovely time playing school with the kitten when she suddenly looked at her watch.

"Goodness me!" she cried. "It's time to collect Boris. Someone who hates school won't like to be kept waiting."

But when Maisie and the kitten arrived, instead of an elephant who hated school, there was a proud, smiling elephant who didn't even notice them at first.

"Well," said Maisie, "how do you like school?"
    But Boris wasn't even listening. He was too busy showing
the kitten how he could turn into a tree.